My Chair

First published in 2010
by Wayland

Text copyright © Louise John
Illustration copyright © Andy Elkerton

Wayland
338 Euston Road
London NW1 3BH

Wayland Australia
Level 17/207 Kent Street
Sydney, NSW 2000

Series Editor: Louise John
Editor: Katie Powell
Cover design: Paul Cherrill
Design: D.R.ink
Consultant: Shirley Bickler

A CIP catalogue record for this book is available from the British Library.

ISBN 9780750260084

Printed in China

Wayland is a division of Hachette Children's Books,
an Hachette UK Company

www.hachette.co.uk

My Chair

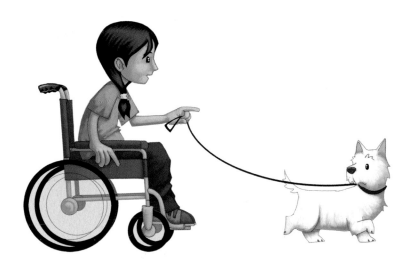

Written by Louise John
Illustrated by Andy Elkerton

WAYLAND

Look at me!

Look at me in my chair.

Look! I can play tag
in my chair.

Look! I can play ball
in my chair.

9

Look! I can dance
in my chair.

Look! I can watch
football in my chair.

13

Look! I can walk the dog in my chair.

Look! I can bake a cake
in my chair.

17

Look! I can have a party in my chair.

19

Look at me!

Look at me in my chair.

21

Guiding a First Read of
My Chair

It is important to talk through the book with the child before they read it alone. This prepares them for the way the story unfolds, and allows them to enjoy the pictures as you both talk naturally, using the language they will later encounter when reading. Read them the brief overview below, and then follow the suggestions.

1. Talking through the book
This girl is in a wheelchair, but she can still do lots of the things that you can do.

> **Let's read the title: My Chair**
> **Look at the pictures.**
> **On page 4, the girl says, "Look at me in my chair!"**
> **Turn over the page and let's see what she can do.**
> **Look! She says, "I can play tag in my chair."**
> **And on the next page, "I can play ball."**

Continue through the book, guiding the discussion to fit the text as the child looks at the illustrations.

> **On page 16, she says, "I can bake a cake."**
> **Why is she doing that? Look on the next page.**
> **Yes, she says, "I can have a party in my chair."**
> **She looks very happy on the last page, doesn't she?**

2. A first reading of the book

Ask the child to read the book independently, pointing carefully under each word (tracking), while thinking about the story. Praise attempts by the child to correct themselves, and prompt them to use their letter knowledge, the punctuation and check the meaning, for example:

I like the way you are pointing under each word.

Good. You checked the picture and she is chasing the other girl. They can play tag, can't they? Now read it again and check if it is 'chasing' or 'tag'.

Well done. I like the way you made her sound happy.

3. Follow-up activities

The high frequency words in this title are:

can   I   in   look   my

- Select a new high frequency word, and ask the child or group to find it throughout the book. Discuss the shape of the letters and the letter sounds.
- To memorise the word, ask the child to write it in the air, then write it repeatedly on a whiteboard or on paper, leaving a space between each attempt.

4. Encourage

- Reading the book again – with expression.
- Drawing a picture based on the story.
- Writing one or two sentences using the practised words.

START READING is a series of highly enjoyable books for beginner readers. **The books have been carefully graded to match the Book Bands widely used in schools.** This enables readers to be sure they choose books that match their own reading ability.

Look out for the Band colour on the book in our Start Reading logo.

The Bands are:

	Pink Band 1A & 1B
	Red Band 2
	Yellow Band 3
	Blue Band 4
	Green Band 5
	Orange Band 6
	Turquoise Band 7
	Purple Band 8
	Gold Band 9

START READING books can be read independently or shared with an adult. They promote the enjoyment of reading through satisfying stories supported by fun illustrations.

Louise John is really the editor of Start Reading, but wanted to see how she liked writing books, too. It was quite tricky, but she found that eating lots of chocolate biscuits made her think better! She tries out her ideas on her daughter, Amelia, who tells her if they are any good or not!

Andy Elkerton spent three years at art college before becoming an artist in the world of computer games. Eventually he escaped and now spends his time illustrating children's books like these.